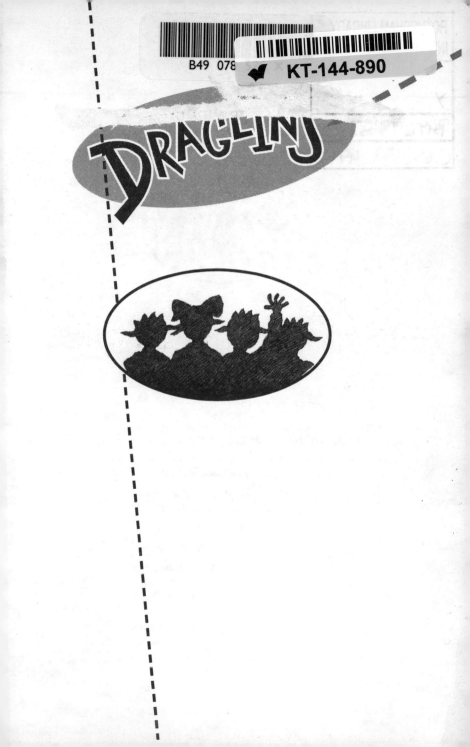

For darling Jack
xx VF

For my mum.
Love, Chris

ORCHARD BOOKS
338 Euston Road, London NW1 3BH
Orchard Books Australia
Level 17/207, Kent Street, Sydney, NSW 2000
First published in Great Britain in 2007
First paperback publication 2008
Text © copyright Vivian French 2007
Illustrations © copyright Chris Fisher 2007
The rights of Vivian French and Chris Fisher to be
identified as the author and illustrator of this work
have been asserted by them in accordance with
the Copyright, Designs and Patents Act, 1988.

A CIP catalogue record for this book is
available from the British Library.

ISBN   978 1 84362 697 8 (hardback)
ISBN   978 1 84362 706 7 (paperback)

1 3 5 7 9 10 8 6 4 2 (hardback)
1 3 5 7 9 10 8 6 4 2 (paperback)
Printed in Great Britain

Orchard Books is a division of Hachette Children's Books,
an Hachette Livre UK company.
www.orchardbooks.co.uk

DRAGLINS TO THE RESCUE!

VIVIAN FRENCH   CHRIS FISHER

ORCHARD BOOKS

CHAPTER ONE

It was very early in the morning.

Danny opened his eyes, and couldn't remember where he was. He stared at the low ceiling, the tiny window, the birch bark walls – and then let out a long happy whistle.

He'd remembered. He and his family had moved. He wasn't in boring old Under Roof any more. Not only had they moved, they'd moved to Uncle Plant and Uncle Puddle's house, and the house was OUTDOORS. Outdoors, where all kinds of adventures were possible.

What was more, he and Dennis had been given their very own mowser. They'd spent all the day before taking turns riding her and feeding her seeds and nuts from Uncle Puddle's secret store cupboard until Uncle Puddle had caught them.

Uncle Puddle had not been pleased. Danny shifted uncomfortably on his sleeping mat as he remembered just how extremely not pleased Uncle Puddle had been. Dennis had shrugged it off, as usual, but Danny decided it wasn't worth risking upsetting Uncle Puddle ever again. Well, not unless it was for a quite extraordinarily good reason.

Danny yawned, and looked at Dennis who was asleep with his mouth open. It was too good an opportunity to miss. Danny peeled a piece of bark off the wall, and flicked it across the room.

"M m m w o o o m
W O O O M P H ! "
spluttered Dennis.
He rolled over,
sat up, and threw
himself at Danny.
They wrestled happily
as the sun rolled higher
into the sky, and the birds began to sing.

Next door Dora lay curled into a ball, her
blanket pulled over her head. Beside her
Daffodil was sleeping peacefully, looking as
if she hadn't a care in the world.

Dora sighed heavily. Everything was
strange. Even the smell of the blanket was
unfamiliar. All her clothes and her few little
possessions were far, far away, bundled up
in a plastic wash bag, and swinging from
a bent nail at the top of a tall high building.

"I'll never see my feather collection again,"
she thought sadly, "or my lovely LOVELY
piece of red wool. ALL my best things are
in that horrid old bag…"

Everybody else's things were there too, but Uncle Damson and Aunt Plum and Daffodil and her brothers didn't seem to mind. Dora did. She was homesick for the high dusty roof space that had been her home for so long, and she wished more than anything that she was safely back there.

Dora pulled the blanket more tightly round her. Things hadn't gone right from the moment the draglins left Under Roof.

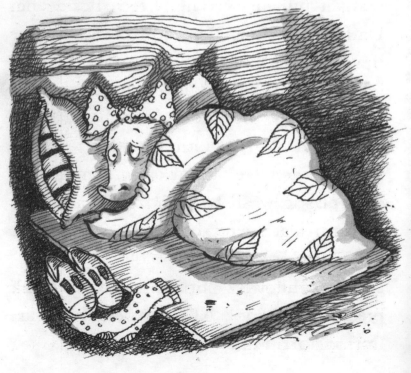

Her heart beat faster as she remembered the dreadful moment when Daffodil had vanished into the terrifying world of Outdoors. Finding her sister safe and sound hadn't made Dora feel any safer. As far as she was concerned, Outdoors was crawling with danger.

She was even afraid of her two newly discovered uncles, Uncle Plant and Uncle Puddle. They had done their best to make Dora and her family feel welcome in Under Shed, but Dora still blushed every time she spoke to them. And the way Uncle Puddle had shouted at Danny and Dennis! Dora shuddered. Why, she'd almost thought she'd seen SMOKE coming out of Uncle Puddle's nostrils, and everyone knew that smoking was the most dreadful thing a draglin could ever EVER do.

Dora swallowed hard, and tried to think Encouraging Thoughts. At least she had Daffodil sharing a sleeping place with her, even if Daffodil did think the whole terrible journey had been one huge excitement from beginning to end. And Dennis and Danny, her brothers, were on the other side of the wall. They were just as excited about moving to a new home as Daffodil, but at least there was a kind of safety in numbers. Uncle Damson and Aunt Plum and little cousin Pip were across the corridor, and, Dora told herself, Aunt Plum and Uncle Damson were experienced grown-up Collectors who knew all about this scary new world. She began to breathe a little more easily.

SCRITCH SCRATCH!

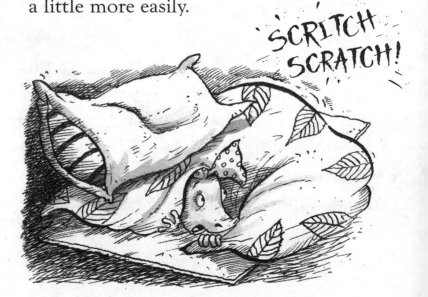

Dora gave a loud wail, and burrowed into the blanket more deeply. She was about to be eaten alive by a dawg – she just knew it. Or a chat. Or even – her heart almost stopped – a Human Beanie.

CHAPTER TWO

The scratching grew louder. Daffodil opened her eyes, sat up, and thumped on the wall.

Dennis's voice said, "Are you awake? I've got a PLAN!"

"Dora! Dora – WAKE UP!" Daffodil bounded across and tugged Dora's blanket away. "Dennis has a plan!"

"What sort of plan?" Dora asked anxiously.

"Don't know," Daffodil said. "Come on! Let's find out!" And she skipped out of the room.

Dora sighed, and slowly followed her sister into Dennis and Danny's room.

Even after just three days Dennis and Danny's room looked as if they'd lived there for ever. There were piles of Useful Sticks, and heaps of Interesting Stones, and a collection of shrivelled leaves, withered berries, and several snail shells. Under Roof had had nothing in it but dust and a few spiders. Outdoors, on the other hand, was an endless source of the most fascinating things Danny and Dennis had ever seen.

Daffodil and Dora edged their way into the room, and found their brothers fully dressed.

"Haven't you got your clothes on yet?"
Dennis sounded astonished. "You'll have to
hurry! We've got to go before the uncles and
Aunt Plum wake up!"

"Go where?" Daffodil asked. A huge smile
spread over her face. "Are we going to hunt
for chats?"

Dennis shook his head. "No." Then, before Dora could heave a sigh of relief, he went on, "Well, not unless we meet some on the way. If we do, we'll tweak their wickers! Yah! Boo! Silly old chats!"

Danny saw Daffodil was about to explode with impatience. "We're going to rescue the wash bag," he explained. "We're going to go to Over Roof, and get it back! Dennis says that'll show Uncle Puddle we're not – what was it he said, Dennis?"

"'Thoughtless and selfish,'" Dennis said indignantly.

"That's right," said Danny. "And it'll show Uncle Damson that we can be Collectors too, just like him and Aunt Plum. SOOPER DOOPER Collectors."

"COOL!" Daffodil said. "Come on, Dor – let's get dressed!"

For once, Daffodil was speedier at getting dressed than Dora.

"Do hurry UP, Dor!" she said, her voice muffled as she struggled into her T-shirt.

"We've got to GO!"

Dora stopped buttoning up her skirt. "Go where?"

"Oh, DORA!" Daffodil's furious head popped out like a cork from a bottle. "Dennis SAID! We're going to rescue our stuff! Now come ON! And don't forget to whisper when we go down the hall!"

Dora nodded. It didn't feel like the right moment to point out that Daffodil was far more likely to wake the grown-ups than she was.

CHAPTER THREE

The four little draglins tiptoed out of Under Shed. Loud snores told them the uncles were still fast asleep, and smaller squeakier snores meant Aunt Plum and Pip were too. Dennis, Daffodil, and Danny closed the front door carefully behind them, and crept away with a feeling of relief.

Only Dora, pulled by Daffodil and pushed from behind by Danny, was horribly disappointed. She'd been hoping and hoping that Aunt Plum would hear them, and come storming out to tell them they were to stay at home for ever and ever. Now it was looking as if she'd have to have yet another adventure, and Dora was quite sure that moving house was as much of an adventure as she could ever want.

"Are we going down the Underground?" she asked Danny.

Danny nodded. "Yes. But we're going to get the mowser first."

"AND we'll take Speedy with us," Daffodil said. "He's MY pet beetle, and he'll be lonely without me."

"But he doesn't do as he's told," Dennis objected.

This was true. Speedy had been sent to live in an outhouse, as he had made Aunt Plum drop Uncle Plant's very best pie dish by scuttling up the wall and into the kitchen cupboards. Uncle Plant said Speedy would be better behaved after Daffodil had trained him, but in the meantime Aunt Plum had said Not In This House. Not Ever.

Daffodil made a face at Dennis, but for once she didn't argue. Instead she pushed her way to the front, and when they reached the mowser's hole she opened the door with a flourish. When Dennis said, "Get out of the WAY, Daffy," she stuck out her tongue, then went to say goodbye to her beetle.

The mowser was more than happy to come on an outing. She had realised that Dennis and Danny always brought her delicious things to eat, so she let Dennis put her harness on with no fuss at all.

"There!" Dennis said proudly as he swung himself onto the mowser's back. "Isn't she GREAT? Now – let's head for the Underground!"

"You won't be able to ride in there," Danny said crossly. He'd wanted to harness the mowser himself. "The roof's not high enough. You'll bump your head and it'll serve you right!"

Daffodil reappeared. "SHHHH!" she said loudly. "Stop ARGUING! Let's go!"

"We don't actually have to go now this minute," Dora said. "We ought to leave Aunt Plum a note so she doesn't worry."

"She won't," Daffodil giggled. "I've made sure Aunt Plum won't worry about us at all."

"Quick as you can," Dennis ordered. "One, two, three – GO!" And he shook the mowser's reins. The mowser squeaked, dashed across the grass, and disappeared into the dark hole that was the entrance to the Underground.

"Wait for me!" yelled Daffodil, and she ran after Dennis.

Danny looked at Dora. "Coming?" he asked. Dora gulped, and nodded. Much as she would have loved to have said No, she knew she couldn't. Wasn't she the sensible one? The one who looked after the others?

Dora took a deep breath, and ran. As the cool darkness of the Underground swallowed her up she was almost certain she could hear Aunt Plum's voice calling from Under Shed, but before she could turn round Danny arrived in a flurry behind her.

"WOW!" he said. "Didn't know you could run so fast, Dor! I couldn't catch you!"

Dora glowed with pleasure, and forgot about Aunt Plum.

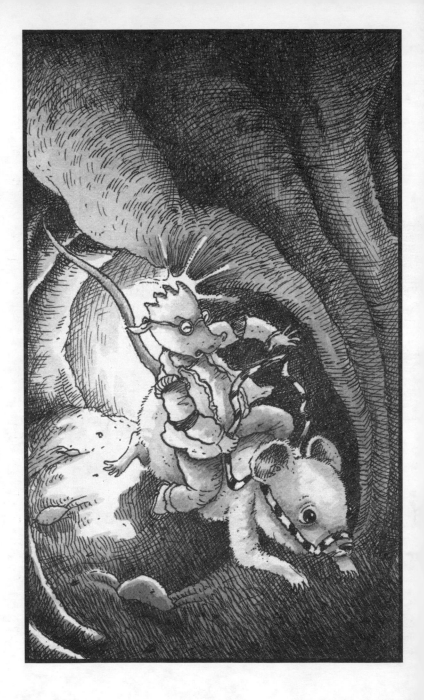

CHAPTER FOUR

"OW!" Dennis bumped his head for the third time. Danny had been right – the Underground roof was very low.

"Oh BOTHER," he said, and slid to the ground. The mowser stopped at once, and Dennis grabbed the reins and waited for his brother and sisters.

"You could have waited by the entrance," Daffodil complained as she came puffing up. "You don't have to show off ALL the time."

"I'm here now, aren't I?" Dennis said, and then as Danny and Dora appeared he went on, "Right. You've got to stay close behind me. Do you remember when we came along here before? There are loads of turnings off, and we don't want to go the wrong way."

"But how will we know which is the right way?" Dora asked.

Dennis looked extraordinarily pleased with himself. "LOOK!" he said, and pointed to the tunnel wall, and a faint row of scratches. "I did it when we were coming here!" he said proudly. "I KNEW we'd want to use the Underground without the grown-ups, so I scratched zigzags with a bit of old brick every time Uncle Damson wasn't looking!"

There was a moment of respectful silence.

"That's VERY clever, Dennis," Dora said at last.

"I know," Dennis said. Then, to Daffodil's disgust, he added, "I'm the cleverest draglin in the whole wide world!" And he led the mowser off down the tunnel.

Daffodil, Danny and Dora trotted behind him, Daffodil muttering to herself. Every so often when the tunnel widened she tried to squeeze by the mowser, but there was never quite enough room. The mowser was elderly and stout, and even though Daffodil was the skinniest of the four little draglins she couldn't get past the big furry bottom in front of her.

"I BET that's why Dennis wanted to bring her," she thought crossly to herself. "He's just a horrible boastful show-off!"

A widening at a right hand bend gave her her opportunity. She slid round the mowser and sprinted past the surprised Dennis, calling, "Gotcha!" Then she hurried on, checking the scratches on the walls as she went.

"Wait!" Dennis yelled. He tried to catch her up, but the mowser refused to go any faster.

"DAFFODIL!" he shouted, "COME BACK!" but all he got was an echoing, "See you later..."

Behind him Dora wailed, "Oh nooooo..."

CHAPTER FIVE

O nce Daffodil was well out of Dennis's sight she slowed down. It was interesting, she thought, that the Underground was never completely dark – there was always a faint glimmer of light from a grating up above, or a side tunnel. It suddenly struck Daffodil that whoever had built it had known exactly what they were doing.

"WOW!" she said to herself. "There must have been HUNDREDS of draglins to build this! Wonder where they all went to? And they must have been REALLY clever – MUCH cleverer than Dennis!" And she hurried on towards a clearer light that she was sure marked the Exit, the Exit that was nearest to the tall high building that had been their home until only three days ago.

The light got brighter and brighter. Daffodil ran faster, and was just about to pop out of the round brick hole at the end when she heard noises. There was a clanking, then a clattering, and finally an incredible CRASH!

As the rumbling faded, clouds of dust flooded the tunnel. Daffodil sneezed, and wiped her eyes. Then came the sound of voices. LOUD voices. Human Beanie voices.

And the Beanies were so close that Daffodil could see them stamping to and fro on the path at the bottom of the grassy slope where the Underground entrance was hidden.

Daffodil was fascinated. She'd never ever seen a real live Beanie before, and nothing had prepared her for the size of them. They were HUGE! The Underground was half way up the slope, but she was still only at the level of the biggest Beanie's waist. All she could see was his dusty trousers, and his clumping boots. Very carefully she edged forwards.

"That's the slates off, Mac," said a booming voice. "Better get them tidied up. Roof beams'll be sent down next. Rotten as anything, those beams."

Daffodil quivered with excitement. She could understand Beanie talk! Forgetting all about Uncle Damson's tales of terror and destruction, she crept outside.

There were hundreds of broken slates lying in heaps on the path, and as Daffodil stared one of the Beanies bent down to shovel them away.

She let out a tiny squeak as she saw his head and shoulders, but the noise of the scraping shovel was much too loud for her to be heard.

The Beanie's face was bright red, and its eyes were bulging as it worked. There were black bristles over its eyes, and more bristles all over its head, and as Daffodil stared it opened its mouth, showing a set of ferocious looking sharp white teeth.

It was muttering and huffing and puffing as it heaved massive heaps of slates into a wheelbarrow, and it smelt hot and nasty. Daffodil was just about to retreat into the safety of the tunnel when something brightly coloured caught her eye.

IT WAS THE PLASTIC WASH BAG!

And it was lying not much more than a quick sprint away from the entrance of the Underground.

Daffodil forgot about the unpleasantness of Human Beanies, and began to think furiously. The wash bag had been left hanging at the top of the building when the family had moved. Uncle Damson's plan to fill it with the family's belongings and push it out of a hole in the roof had failed miserably, because the bag had caught on a nail – but the collapse of the slates must have swept it down to ground level. An idea floated into Daffodil's head, and a gleeful smile spread across her face.

"I'll tell them I FETCHED the bag!" She hugged herself for being so clever. "I'll tell them I climbed up, and then pushed it down and jumped after it – oops! Here they are! Just WAIT until they see that wash bag!"

Her ears twitched as she heard Dennis and the others tiptoeing along the tunnel behind her, and she gave a little skip.

And then she heard a Beanie's voice booming, "What's that along there, Nige? Chuck it here, will you?" And the shovelling Beanie straightened himself, strode over to the wash bag, and picked it up.

CHAPTER SIX

Daffodil staggered back from the entrance. Dennis, who had spent most of the journey practising the horrible things he was going to say to her, forgot them when he saw her face. Danny and Dora pushed past the mowser, and Dora ran to Daffodil to hug her.

"What is it?" she asked nervously. "Oh Daffy – what's happened? Why ever are you looking like that, and why are you covered in dust?"

Daffodil waved her arms dramatically. "A Human Beanie's got our wash bag!" she said. "He's out there now – listen!"

Dennis, Danny and Dora froze as the tunnel was filled with the echoing roar of a Beanie voice.

"Nothing in here but rubbish. Some kid's stuff, by the look of it. Might keep the bag, though. The wife might like it."

"Fancy a break, Mac?" It was the other Beanie talking now, the one called Nige. "I've got a flask of coffee in the van."

There was a splintering sound as the heavy feet stamped over the slates, and then silence. Dora stopped holding her breath. She looked at Daffodil, her eyes very wide. "Have you SEEN them, Daffy?"

Daffodil nodded in what she hoped was a casual sort of way. "Oh yes," she said. "I've been watching them for ages."

"Are they AWFUL?" Dora wanted to know.

"They're OK," Daffodil said.

"What are they like?" Danny asked.

Daffodil suddenly got bored with pretending she wasn't at all impressed by the Beanies. "HUGE!" she said. "And HORRIBLE! And they SMELL!"

"Here," Dennis said, and he pushed Danny towards the mowser. "Hold her a minute. I want to see!" And he crept to the entrance and looked out. Daffodil immediately followed him, and Danny thrust the mowser's reins into Dora's hands and rushed after her.

"WOW!" said Dennis as he squinted upwards. "LOOK! There isn't any roof! It's just beams up there!"

"It's a good thing we moved when we did," Danny said.

"I could have hidden away," Daffodil boasted. "They didn't see me just now, and I was so near I could see the bristles on their heads!"

"YUCK!" said Danny. "That's GROSS!"

Dennis was listening to the Outside. "It doesn't sound as if there's anyone near here..." he said, and he pushed his way out through the grass and onto the slope. The light was very bright, and he rubbed his eyes as he stared at the building rubble, the wheelbarrow, and the abandoned shovel. Then he saw a wisp of red.

"HEY!" he called. "QUICK! Come and look!"

Daffodil was already beside him. "It's Dora's wool! That was in the wash bag!" Before Dennis could say anything she was scampering off to fetch it. Dennis ran after her, but Danny hesitated for a moment. He was sure there were Beanies still working on the roof.

"Dora!" he whispered. "Can you keep watch? If you see ANY Beanies at all, whistle as loudly as you can!"

Dora let out a terrified squeal. "But I don't WANT to see a Beanie!"

"None of us does," Danny said. "But Daffodil's found our things!"

Danny was right. Hidden from the entrance hole by a heap of slates were the contents of the wash bag. The Mac Beanie must have shaken the bag until it was empty. Sleeping mats, clothes, pots, pans and all kinds of draglin household goods were scattered far and wide.

Daffodil and Dennis were rushing here and there, picking things up and then dropping them as they tried to carry more.

"That's no good," Danny said. "We need something to collect them in. Here!" He grabbed one of Uncle Damson's large nightshirts. "Stuff the clothes in this. Look —" he pushed a pillowcase towards Daffodil. "You can use that!"

"WOW!" Daffodil was looking inside a box. "These must be all our baby clothes!"

"DAFFODIL! You haven't got time to open things! The Beanies will be back any minute!" Danny seized an armful of clothes and stuffed them inside the nightshirt. He began dragging it back to the Underground, and Dennis walked beside him with three sleeping mats balanced on top of his head.

"Look!" he said. "I bet I can carry them with no hands!"

The sleeping mats slid off.

Daffodil immediately sat on them, laughing.

"Get OFF!" Dennis shouted.

"Make me!" Daffodil said cheerfully.

"Stop messing about," Danny told them. "We've still got loads to pick up—"

EEEEEEEE EEEEEEEEE!

It was a whistle – Dora's loudest whistle.

At the same moment there was the sound of loud Beanie voices, and the thump! thump! thump! of Beanie boots.

"RUN!" yelled Danny, and the three little draglins ran.

CHAPTER SEVEN

To Dora, twitching in the Underground, it seemed an age until her brothers and Daffodil flung themselves in through the entrance. The mowser had been squeaking anxiously, but when she saw Dennis and Danny she began to frisk about. Dora suddenly realised what was wrong with her.

"She's HUNGRY!" she said.

Danny dug in his pockets, and brought out a couple of dried berries. The mowser swallowed them at a gulp, and snuffled for more.

"She'll have to wait," Dennis said over his shoulder. He was peering through the grass. "Those two huge Beanies are back. One of them's started shovelling the slates up again. The other one's just standing scratching his head. Now he's waving his arms –

I think it's some kind of non-talk Beanie language. He's waving again. Oh, now I can see Beanies on the top of the roof. They're waving too. HEY! The Beanies outside are going again. Wow! Look! They're running! Hurrah! We can go back and get our things!" And Dennis hopped away before anyone could stop him. Daffodil shot after him, determined she was going to be in on the action.

At once there was a deafening roar as the roof beams came thundering down from the top of the building.

The "THUMP!" as the rotten wood hit the ground made the Underground shake. The mowser let out a terrified squeal, pulled free of her reins, and rushed away. Dora shrieked and clutched at Danny, and Danny gasped and shut his eyes as the earth beneath his feet trembled.

When Danny opened his eyes again it was pitch dark. "Dor?" he whispered. "Are you really OK?"

"I don't know," Dora sobbed. "What's happened, Danny? Are we dead?"

"No," Danny said. "But the Underground entrance is all blocked up. That's why it's so dark."

"Dennis and Daffy were out there!" Dora's sobs grew louder. "Oh, Danny – they're SURE to be dead! They must have been squished and squashed! I KNEW we shouldn't have come!"

Danny didn't answer. He thought he was beginning to see a faint glimmer of daylight.

"Give me your hand, Dor," he said. "Look – come this way."

The two little draglins crept towards the cracks of light. They were getting brighter all the time, and Danny realised that although there was a huge wooden beam right in front of the entrance he could, if he bent down, catch a tiny glimpse of the grass beyond, thick with dust. As he squinted out a shaky voice called, "Danny? Dora?"

"DENNIS!" Danny yelled, and Dora began to scrabble furiously at the wood. "Dennis – are you all right? Where's Daffy?"

"Haven't seen her," Dennis said. "It's a horrible mess out here."

Danny peered through the gloom. The wood was riddled with worm holes, and where Dora was working small chunks were breaking away with little flurries of soft orange sawdust.

"I think we could dig our way out," he said. "Can you try from your side?"

There was a moment's hesitation, and then Dennis said, "Yes."

"NO!" Dora stopped her frenzied scratching. "No – PLEASE go and look for Daffy, Dennis."

"If we can get out we can ALL look," Danny told her. "Come on – you're doing brilliantly, Dora. Let me squeeze in beside you. Looks like that's the weakest bit."

Dora and Danny pulled and tugged and heaved at the rotten wood until they were exhausted. As they stopped to catch their breath, Dora grabbed Danny's arm. "It's gone quiet!" she whispered. "Where's Dennis?"

She was right. There was no sign of any activity on the other side.

"DENNIS?" Danny bent down to look under the beam. "DENNIS! Are you there?"

There was no answer.

"Come on," Danny said grimly. "Get digging! We've GOT to get out there and see what's happening!"

CHAPTER EIGHT

Outside, Dennis was scrambling over splintered wood and sliding down heaps of slates.

"Daffy!" he called. "Daffodil? Where are you?"

There was no answer. Dennis chose a large piece of beam, and climbed to the top so he could look round. On one side he could see the apparently deserted tenement building, and on the other the wreckage of the roof.

"Wow!" he said, as he realised just how many planks were piled up in front of the Underground entrance. "They'll NEVER dig their way through that lot! I'll have to go home Overground – just as soon as I find Daffodil."

A tiny movement much further along the slope caught his eye. "DAFFY?" he yelled, and was mid-leap to the ground when a cross voice said, "SHH! Stop YELLING!

The Human Beanies will hear you and come back!"

Dennis did a spectacular turnaround in mid air. The voice sounded VERY near. "DAFFODIL! Where ARE you?" he called as he landed.

"Underneath you," said the voice.

Dennis bent down and began scooping away soot and cinders and bits of crumbling chimney. Daffodil's head gradually emerged, covered in white plaster dust.

Dennis began to giggle. "You look like a ghost," he said.

"Just get me OUT," Daffodil said. "Here, come on—" she wriggled until she could lift up one of her arms. "Give me a pull!"

Dennis heaved, and Daffodil shot out of the rubble like a jack-in-a-box.

She looked at Dennis. "You're white too," she said. "Where are Danny and Dora?"

Dennis wiped his face. "They're stuck in the tunnel," he said. "We'll have to go home Overground. There's half the roof beams outside the entrance."

"Cool," Daffodil said. "Hey – maybe we'll meet a chat! That would be good!"

"Fantastic!" Dennis agreed. Then he remembered. "Oh – I think I saw something move just now. Right over there – way past where the wood and stuff is. Come and look."

Daffodil followed Dennis onto his look-out position. Together they stared at the grassy slope.

"Hope it's a chat," Daffodil said. "I really want to see—"

"OH!" Dennis grabbed Daffodil's arm. "IT'S THE MOWSER!"

"However did she get there?" Daffodil wondered. "Oh – she's disappeared again!" She rubbed at her dirty nose, and suddenly her eyes lit up.

"DENNIS!" she said. "Do you know what? I bet it's ANOTHER EXIT FROM THE UNDERGROUND!"

Dennis stared at his sister. "GENIUS! Let's go!"

And the two little draglins began scrambling as fast as they could towards the far end of the slope.

Down in the Underground Dora and Danny were still toiling away. They had broken down a large part of the beam in front of the entrance, but the soft rotten wood had given way to a much harder, tougher surface. Danny scraped and scratched as best he could, but made hardly any impression.

"Oh Dor," he said wearily. "We'll NEVER get through this. If only we had something sharp—"

"OUCH!" Dora let out a loud squeal, and sucked her fingers. "Danny, look!"

"Well done!" Danny reached up, and tugged at the rusty nail Dora had uncovered. "That's PERFECT! We'll be out in no time now!" The nail came away more suddenly than Danny had expected, and he

There was a loud giggle from behind. Danny and Dora spun round, hardly daring to believe what they had just heard.

CHAPTER NINE

"You look SO funny!" Daffodil said cheerfully as she dropped a pillowcase, filthy, but stuffed with clothes, onto the ground.

"Yes!" Dennis dumped a pile of sleeping mats on top. "And why are you doing all that digging? Why don't you go to one of the other entrances if you want to get out?"

Danny and Dora stared at him without moving.

Dennis came closer, and smiled an Aren't-I-Clever smile. "You didn't guess, did you?" he said. "WE did. All those passages leading off – they go to all kinds of different places. Daffy and I are planning all SORTS of adventures—"

Dora sat down and began to cry.

Danny threw down his rusty nail and glared furiously at Dennis.

"We were digging to try and rescue you!" he shouted. "Why didn't you SAY you were going to look for another entrance? We've been scared out of our heads because we thought you were DEAD! You're HORRIBLE, both of you — you spoil everything and I NEVER want to go on an adventure with you again!" And Danny sat down beside Dora with his back to Dennis and Daffodil.

There was a long awkward silence.

"Sorry," Dennis said at last.

"Yes," said Daffodil. "We didn't think."

"You never DO," Danny said crossly.

Daffodil made a face, and wandered off down the tunnel.

Dora blew her nose hard, and stood up. "Let's go home," she said. A sudden thought struck her. "Oh, Dennis. Something awful happened! The mowser ran away, and I don't know where she is. I'm so sorry. When the wood came crashing down it was TERRIFYING, and she was so scared she just zoomed off."

"That's OK," Dennis said in a very offhand way. Danny peered at him through the gloom.

"OK?" he said. "What do you mean, OK? She was my mowser too, you know! We'll have to find her." He gave Dennis a sour smile. "She could be ANYWHERE! We could have been looking for her if we hadn't been trying to get to YOU."

"But she's here!" Daffodil said chirpily.

"We found her outside the other exit! We tied her to a root, and picked up all the bits and pieces we could find, and then we came back!"

A smile slowly spread over Danny's face.

"THAT'S how you found your way back, isn't it? You didn't REALLY know about the other entrances and exits – you saw the mowser coming out! THAT'S how you found a way back in! You didn't find HER – she found YOU!"

Daffodil nodded. "Yes. Why?"

"Because that means Dennis isn't the Mr Clever he pretends to be," Danny said with some satisfaction. "And I'M going to lead the mowser on the way back. Oh—" he looked at Dora " – unless you want to, Dor. You've been working harder than anyone."

Dora beamed, but shook her head. "We could put the sleeping mats and the other things on the mowser's back," she suggested. "If she doesn't mind, that is." She stroked the mowser's head. "She's SO clever..."

"Good thinking!"
Dennis said
enthusiastically.
"Then we won't
have to carry
anything!"

Dora looked
doubtfully at the
grubby heap piled
on the Underground
floor. "I do hope Uncle Damson and Aunt
Plum will be pleased," she said.

"Of course they will. And it'll stop them
telling us off. It'll be FINE, Dor," Daffodil
promised.

"What?" Dora stared at her sister. "But
you said you'd made sure Aunt Plum
wouldn't worry!"

Daffodil grinned a wicked grin. "I said
she'd be too busy to worry about us!
I let my beetle out...and Uncle Damson left
the kitchen window open last night. It won't
be my fault if Speedy climbs inside!"

"DAFFY! Aunt Plum will be FURIOUS! He made a HORRIBLE mess last time!" Dora was deeply shocked, but Daffodil took no notice. She helped Danny heave the last sleeping mat onto the mowser's back, and took Dora's arm.

"Come on, fusspot," she said fondly. "Let's get home. I'm REALLY hungry!"

"I've still got some berries," Dennis said, but as he fished in his pockets Dora stepped forward, her eyes flashing.

"You should give those to the mowser!" she said. "It's the mowser that deserves them. If it hadn't been for her, you'd never have found your way back, and we'd still be trying to dig our way out – and we'd probably ALL have ended up being eaten by Human Beanies!"

There was a small pause, and then Dennis gave the berries to the mowser.

"Well said, Dora," Danny said.

Daffodil nodded.

CHAPTER TEN

They made the journey back through the Underground without any difficulties. The mowser knew exactly which way to go, so there was no need to look at Dennis's marks on the walls as they walked steadily along.

It was only when they could see the bright sunshine showing the way out to their new home in Under Shed that silence fell. Dora was worrying about what Uncle Damson and Aunt Plum would say, and Danny had been thinking for at least five minutes of the awfulness of Uncle Puddle in a rage.

Daffodil and Dennis braved it out until the end, but even Daffodil felt a sudden twinge of nervousness as the mowser trotted out into the daylight. For once she didn't try to push to the front –

she let Dora and Danny and the mowser hurry across the short space from the Underground exit, and then followed with Dennis.

The house was very quiet. There was no sign of any of the uncles, or Aunt Plum and Pip. Danny and Dennis put the mowser back in her hole, and came out to find Daffodil leaning over the door of her beetle's shed.

"He's back inside!" she said. "Do you think the uncles caught him?"

"Let's hope he didn't wreck the kitchen first," Dennis said.

"Daffy! Danny! Dennis!" It was Dora calling. "I've had SUCH a good idea!"

The others looked at each other. "Probably hard work," Daffodil sighed. "Come on – we'd better see what she wants."

Dora was waiting by the front door. "Nobody's here," she said, "so why don't we sort out the stuff from Under Roof?

Lots of it needs washing, but we could arrange the pans in the kitchen, and put the sleeping mats out."

Dennis groaned, but he grabbed a sleeping mat and carried it off. Danny picked up a piece of paper that was lying behind the door.

"Hey!" he said. "They've left us a note!" He let out a loud whoop. "YEAH! They thought we'd rushed off to find Daffy's beetle. Oh – Uncle Puddle caught him trying to climb in the window just before they had to go out! And – guess what? Uncle Plant's put a PS saying he's glad we took the mowser because she's got some sense even if we haven't!"

All four little draglins relaxed. Dora went on pottering about putting things in their places, but the others flopped onto the sofa.

"I'm tired," Danny yawned.

"I'm HUNGRY," Dennis said, and at that moment they heard the sounds of their family coming through the door.

"Hello," Aunt Plum said as she hurried inside. "I'm SO sorry we've been so long. I do hope you weren't worried!"

"We were fine, thank you," Daffodil said with her sweetest smile.

Uncle Damson looked at her suspiciously. "What have you been up to?"

"Nothing," Daffodil said, but Aunt Plum had seen the row of saucepans on the cooker.

"My PANS!" she gasped, and then she saw the heap of dirty clothes. "And your CLOTHES! OH! Oh, that's WONDERFUL! Wherever did they come from?"

Dennis, Danny, Daffodil and Dora swelled with pride.

"We've been Collecting," Dennis said. "Just for you."

Aunt Plum's eyes opened very wide, but she said nothing. Uncle Damson stared at the little draglins, and went an astonishing shade of purple.

"You've been WHAT?" he exploded, but before he could say anything more Uncle Puddle grabbed his arm.

"Well DONE, Damson!" he boomed.

"That's RIGHT!" echoed Uncle Puddle. "We never realised you'd got 'em trained already!"

"And dashed good at it, I'd say," Uncle Puddle went on. "Look at them! Safely back, so they must have looked after each other." He turned to the four astonished draglins. "Excellent! And we've got something for you." He went to the door, and whistled.

A tiny mowser, hardly more than a baby, crept into the room. Dora's eyes shone, and there was a universal "Ahhhhhhhhh!"

"There you are, young Dora!" said Uncle Plant. "Said we'd get you a pet of your own!"

"THANK YOU!" breathed Dora. "She's BEAUTIFUL!"

"You'll have to find a name for her," Aunt Plum said.

"Can we help choose?" Daffodil asked eagerly, and Dora nodded.

"You know what?" Uncle Plant said suddenly. "The old mowser doesn't have a name. Any ideas?"

Dora didn't hesitate for a second.

"Hero," she said.

Uncle Puddle raised an eyebrow. "Do I ask why?"

"Better not," said Daffodil, and she grinned.

Aunt Plum inspected her nephews and nieces. They all seemed remarkably cheerful, even Dora...but they were VERY dirty.

"Right!" she said briskly. "Time for a bath!" And as Daffodil, Dennis and Danny groaned loudly she put her arm round Dora. "Not too homesick?" she asked.

Dora nodded. "I was," she said, "but it's odd. I'm not now. I suppose you can't be homesick for something that isn't there any more, can you?" And she skipped off to the bathroom to make sure that Daffodil washed her neck.

"Well well," said Uncle Damson. "Wonders will never cease."

"No," said Aunt Plum. And then she added a little nervously, "But whatever will they get up to next?"

by Vivian French
illustrated by Chris Fisher

All priced at £3.99.

Draglins books are available from all good bookshops,
or can be ordered direct from the publisher:
Orchard Books, PO BOX 29, Douglas IM99 1BQ.
Credit card orders please telephone 01624 836000
or fax 01624 837033 or visit our website:
www.orchardbooks.co.uk
or e-mail: bookshop@enterprise.net for details.

To order please quote title, author and ISBN
and your full name and address.
Cheques and postal orders should be made
payable to 'Bookpost plc.'

Postage and packing is FREE within the UK
(overseas customers should add £2.00 per book).

Prices and availability are subject to change.